Francis Dingwall obtained an English degree from Oxford University, and then qualified as a solicitor.

In his legal career, he specialises as a 'lawyer for lawyers', defending Professional Negligence claims for solicitors and other professionals, and advising law firms on how to keep – and get – out of trouble. Along the way, he spent two years working as a Parliamentary Counsel drafting legislation. He has been a member in Legal Risk LLP since 2007.

He obtained an Undergraduate Diploma in Creative Writing from Oxford University in 2005, and since then he has written a children's novel and short stories.

Legal Risk LLP is the law firm to whom lawyers themselves turn for help, a niche firm of solicitors. The firm specialises in providing legal advice to law firms on (1) Professional Discipline, and (2) Professional Liability. Much of the work consists of advising firms in trouble, but we also advise firms how to achieve their ambitions without breaking the ever-changing rules.

Clients include 30 of the Top 100 UK law firms, plus leading US firms and European practices. The firm also act for law firms of different shapes and sizes, and has acted for over 500 firms in the 14 years since it was established.

Francis Dingwall

Cautionary Tales

lessons in ethics for lawyers

Legal Risk LLP

All rights reserved

Published by Legal Risk LLP, 28 Bixteth Street, Liverpool L3 9UH.

© Francis Dingwall 2016

ISBN: 978-1-5262-0433-2

Typeset in Garamond MT

Printed and bound in England by CPI Antony Rowe

Contents

Two Masters

I know solicitors have their conflicts rules, but if I am temping in a firm where they involve the secretaries in opening the file, I apply some extra ones of my own. And one of my rules is that blood relatives require separate lawyers in commercial transactions. I should know: I come from a family of twins.

So I was ready for Amanda when she appeared at my workstation. She squinted down at me through her ice-blue eyes as if I was very small. Or very far away. She did not have her glasses on, and I could not read in the shining lights of those icy eyes whether she had her contacts in.

"Have you opened the file for the Grouses? They're coming in this afternoon."

"The brace of Grice?"

"The what?"

"A pair of gloves, a brace of grouse. Mouse, mice. I was waiting to ask you which one the firm is going to act for. They're cousins, aren't they?"

"What has that got to do with anything?" Her lips pursed into a thin and disdainful wrinkle. The upper lip slightly protruded over the bottom one. A flaw in the diamond.

"I come from a family of twins," I started.

"I don't care if you come from a family of octopuses. I'm acting for both of them. Together. They're buying the pub together."

"Isn't it only the smooth cousin putting in the money?"

"Yes, but he's not 'smooth' as you put it, and anyway the rough one – I mean the other one," she almost smiled, but quickly re-wrinkled her lips, "is going to manage it. It's a joint venture."

"I know, but…". Again she cut me off.

"I told you, I don't want to hear about your twins. It's a joint venture, the clients have a common interest, we can act for them both. This is precisely why secretaries shouldn't use their initiative."

I wouldn't like to share a solicitor with anyone in my family. Thankfully I'm not a twin myself, but I've seen how it works. There's the oafish one who gets into trouble all the time, and the angelic one. When you grow up with them, out of sight of parents and teachers you get to see it's the poker-faced angel prodding the innocent oaf into all that trouble. There are different mixes elsewhere among the cousins, but all roads lead to Rome.

I looked up at Amanda. She was already turning on her stiletto heel, and then without a backward glance she was gone.

Some people say 'Go along and get along'. GAGA I call that. It's not my way. As a temp I have the option to get out instead of get along. So when Amanda had them both in the meeting room that afternoon, and asked me to bring down terms of business for signature, I brought two sets, one addressed to Alistair Grouse, and one addressed to

Marco Grouse. They were already standing, ready to leave, by the time I knocked and let myself in.

There was no family resemblance, except that they were about the same height. One was tall and slim, pale and smooth with smarmed-back hair; I guessed he was Alistair Grouse, the investor. The other was a barrel of a man, ruddy, with a receding wild shock of hair like a clown's; that had to be Marco Grouse. The thin one, Alistair, wore a sleek suit, snug in the collar and long in the sleeves, with polished black Oxfords. The fat one, Marco, wore a blazer, fancy waistcoat, jeans and converse sneakers. He was broader, bulkier, but if it came to a fight between them, I thought, I would bet on the thin one.

"Which set of terms is going to be signed?" I asked. I held them both out to Amanda, one in each hand.

With the clients there, she could only register her irritation through her ice-blue eyes. Or was it her eyesight again? She turned to them both:

"I'm afraid my – she paused – secretary here has overlooked the joint nature of the instruction. He seems to think you're at daggers drawn."

She turned to me.

"We've already discussed this. You'll have to redo the document. We're acting for them both. Joint clients, one file, one set of terms."

The two cousins were looking at me oddly. I have seen that look often enough to know that they were not thinking about conflicts of interest. They were contemplating the notion of a male secretary. Then the smooth one looked away from me to the fat one.

"We're not against one another, are we Marco?" the thin one stated rather than asked.

"No. We want the same thing: the best pub in Westchester. We're Marks and Spencer, Morecombe and Wise!"

"Sure," smiled the thin one. A thin smile.

Amanda turned again to me. "You heard them. Go back upstairs and print out one set of terms for them both, and I really need it down here in no more than two minutes." She turned to them, and apologised for the delay.

By the time I returned, the three of them were standing in Reception. Martha, the receptionist, was handing the thin one his coat. The fat one had no coat, despite the cold. They both signed the terms.

As soon as they were out of the door, Martha turned to Amanda.

"That was a lovely coat, Amanda, cashmere the label said. Worth a bob."

She gave Amanda a private look, excluding me. It was well known that Amanda was one of those beautiful women who is forever single. "You have the thin one," Martha continued, "and I'll take the big one." Martha was not a small woman herself.

"You fancy being a publican's wife, do you?"

"If he owns a pub, I'm in. What does yours do? He doesn't look the type to pull pints."

"He's putting in the money."

The phone started ringing. "Then he's the one for you," said Martha quickly, as she pressed the button on the phone. "Good morning, Bracket & Earnshaw, how can we help you?" in a rich tone which was intended to convey to the caller that the help would not be free.

The matter proceeded. Drafts travelled between the different parties: the Joint Venture Agreement pinging between the cousins, the Sale Agreement and Transfer between the seller's solicitors and Amanda. All travelled via me. Amanda refrained from typing anything herself. "Don't learn to type, or they'll turn you into a typist" had been a guiding principle for graduate women entering the jobs market. Unfortunately for me, it had not been a principle that guided me as a male graduate. Which had started me down the rocky path towards this desk where I sat, transcribing her scribbles. For such a beauty, she had ungirlish, ugly handwriting. An old-fashioned love letter from her would not look treasurable, it would look like a ransom note.

As the amendments to the documents multiplied, Amanda took to standing over me in the secretaries' room, behind me, dictating. There is nothing worse.

The week wore on, and the tracked changes on the JVA outstripped that on all the other documents. As amendments to amendments appeared in different colours, patches of the deed began to look bruised, violet, yellow and green over red, blue and black. Amanda seemed to be spending all her time on the phone. On the Friday, when I went into her room to do her filing – her office was as messy as her handwriting – I caught snatches of her conversations.

"He wants the wishing well cleared out and reinstated …"

A wishing well? I listened on. She was certainly talking to one of the Grouses.

"…If you give that to him, I think he'll agree to everything."

Her voice was soothing, easy on the ear: she was talking to the thin one. I wanted to ask about the wishing well, but she seemed wrapped up in herself.

I filed on, and ten minutes later her the phone went again. This time, she sounded exasperated:

"You're not listening to me, Marco. He's the one putting in the money. It won't happen without him, so you have to compromise …"

"…I know you are, …. I know, it's an equal contribution, but …"

Just as I finished the filing, the phone went again. I could tell it was the fat one.

"You're not listening, Marco. I've already told you."

Amanda signalled to me. She put her hand on the receiver.

"No more calls after this one," she whispered. " It's too much like a battle."

"*Ils ne passeront pas*," I promised.

As the afternoon wore on, it wasn't Marco I had trouble with, but the other, Alistair. He was very persistent, but I held the line.

The following Monday, I was greeted by the statuesque Martha in Reception with a sharp intake of breath.

"You're not popular with Amanda. She wants you in her room."

"Why?"

"You ruined her weekend, you did."

If I had been employed, the summons might have struck a spark of terror in me. But one of the attractions of being a temp is the freedom from the tyranny of having a boss, the freedom to walk on eggshells without worrying if they crunch underfoot.

"Why didn't you tell me Alistair was trying to call me on Friday?" She looked tired, as if she had been working all weekend.

I struggled to remember. Alistair? Alistair Grouse. So she was on first name terms.

"You said you didn't want any calls."

"I didn't mean him. I meant no calls from the other one. Fortunately for you, he got me on my mobile in the end, but only last night. Anyway, I want you to go to the pub today."

I was confused. Why would it ruin her weekend at all? Why did she need to speak to Alistair Grouse on a Sunday? It wasn't that urgent was it? And what was this about the pub: she was not the joking type, and nor did she look in the mood for a joke. In my confusion, I answered:

"It's my lucky day, then."

Amanda pursed her lips. No, she was not joking.

"It's a site meeting in the Grouse matter. Alistair is giving me a lift. I may need you …" – she paused – "… to hold the other end of the measuring tape."

"What are we measuring?"

"The plot at the premises the Grouses are buying, of course."

"When?"

"Now."

Why can't Alistair hold the other end of the tape, I asked myself. It wasn't part of my job description to chaperone the female partners.

Alistair was waiting outside in his car, which matched his suit, his coat, his smarmed down hair. I'm not big on cars, and either it was a Maserati or a Korean copy. Whatever it was, it had very little room in the back, and I was scrunched up. In the front, Alistair and Amanda chatted with an easy familiarity. I felt like a squashed gooseberry. Fortunately, the journey took less than five minutes. When you eliminated the time spent diverted by the one-way system, I realised it was more or less round the corner from the office.

The other cousin, Marco, was waiting at the door with the surveyor and a couple of other men.

"Why's he got them with him?" muttered Alistair. "We agreed it's not going to be refitted."

Amanda had the key. The door stuck. Marco put his bulk against it, and it swung open. He ushered them all in as if he was already 'mine host', with an exaggerated hand signal of welcome. He wore a visionary expression. He did not see the dingy lounge bar as it was, but as it would be newly refurbished and crowded with patrons. He was painting it to them:

"And the dining area will be extended into here, with a 360° glass woodburner here."

"Slow down, cousin, slow down," interjected Alistair, glancing over at Amanda. "We've agreed that the funds for the refit will be released when the turnover reaches £50k a quarter."

"I still say that's the wrong way round. The refit will stimulate demand, it's chicken and egg..."

Amanda stopped him. "We've been over that. It's chicken and egg, I know, but you'll just have to hold on to your vision. You and Alistair have agreed the trigger for the further injection of cash. Let's go and have a look at the garden."

Alistair shepherded the group towards the door. Marco held back.

"Come on," Alistair encouraged him, "let's throw a coin down that wishing well of yours."

Marco's eyes lit up. "Yes, that's our USP: that'll draw in the families. We'll need a kid's menu."

At the far end of the beer garden, we all stood round the well, which was covered with a crosswork of flat bars, and the surveyor shone his torch down it. The torchlight could not penetrate the dark to the bottom. He threw a pebble down. Not a sound. He tried a rock. I forgot to count. A faint chink echoed up. There was no splash.

Marco drew from his pocket a sketch of the structure he was proposing to go on it, a chintzy little roof, wall, bucket and winch.

"You won't be needing the bucket," said the surveyor. "The water table must have shifted."

"Don't spoil the magic," said Amanda. As she complimented the sketch, Alistair broke away from the group and strode away. I looked up. Two men in tweed jackets, white shirts with button-down collars and chinos, were standing at the door into the beer garden, like two Mormons. Now Alistair was speaking to them. Marco stopped talking. They were too far away for us to hear what was being said, and soon they left and Alistair was striding back.

"Who were they?" asked Marco.

"Just a couple of guys from the Planning Department."

"You told me we don't need any planning permission."

"And that's right. And they've gone." He waved his hand, as if waving them magically away.

Amanda spoke.

"Shall we get on with the measuring? The plans don't make it clear where the boundary ends over there." She unfolded a plan and turned to the surveyor. "Looking at the ground, I'd say it follows that old stone wall. Leslie, I wonder if you could hold the other end of the surveyor's measuring tape …"

When we were done, I wanted to walk back to the office, but Alistair insisted on giving Amanda a lift again, and in turn she insisted on me being scrunched in the back. Once moving, he turned to Amanda.

"That was a close shave with the planners. Do you think Marco suspected anything?"

"I've advised him the same as you, Alistair. He knows that if the turnover doesn't reach £100,000 by the end of September, the pub closes and the freehold is yours. What you do with it then is up to you. You know and I know that the Planning Office want to see if the business is viable, before they consider residential use. I'm not under a duty to advise Marco about that."

"Let's just hope he doesn't make too much of a success of it," said Alistair. "I think I know how to make it pretty unlikely."

"I don't think I want to know," said Amanda. "I might have to tell Marco," she teased. "In the meantime, it falls outside the scope of my retainer to inquire."

Her flirting with Alistair fell well outside the scope of her retainer, I thought to myself. What if Marco was entitled to the same level of service!

The next day, Amanda finally told me to remove the tracking on the Joint Venture Agreement. With the click of my mouse, the bruising rounds of amendment and counter-amendment all healed miraculously, leaving a pristine agreement. Another click and the document was engrossed, printed out and ready to be signed.

"Could you call Marco and get him in to sign it?" she

asked.

"What about Alistair?"

"I'll be seeing him later, so I'll get him to sign it then."

Six weeks later Amanda passed me an invitation to the re-opening of the pub. *Wet your whistle at the Wishing Well.*

"Can you do a letter for me, give my apologies, you know the sort of thing to say."

"That was quick, six weeks to refurbish the premises."

"There's been a little unpleasantness over it, unfortunately. Marco struggled with the limits on the budget. But it was as they had agreed. Alistair doesn't think he'll be welcome at the opening, and he thinks it may be better if I don't go either."

Free beer and sandwiches.

"Do you mind if I go? It's only round the corner, so I can fit it into my lunch hour."

"Yes, that would be good, a suitable level of representation from the firm. Just don't get drawn into any discussion on the terms of the deal. Not that he would ask *you*."

She must have had it in her diary, because on the day, immediately after lunch she was at my workstation, asking me how I had got on.

"The beer was average. It was lucky it was free, because you can't compete with the supermarkets on price. The sandwiches were better than supermarket ones, though."

"What about the refurbishment?"

"The garden looks really good, he's done a lot of work on that, but it was raining, so we were stuck inside, and that was a problem, because the interior looked as dingy as before. So I don't know."

"Yes, Ali said Marco spent too much on the garden, and he didn't leave himself enough to redo the interior. He spent £20,000 on his wretched wishing well."

"Mmmm. It's a bit of a Disney wishing well, but maybe kids would like that. On a sunny day, it would be a good family pub."

"Pity it's in England, then! Did he say anything about the firm? Or about me?"

I should have lied, but the beer in me unleashed the truth. "He thinks you're f…," fortunately Amanda's boss – Dan – passed, and by the time he had gone, I had got the truth back on its leash.

"He thinks I'm what?"

"Oh, he thinks you're … fond of his cousin."

"I need you to do some urgent typing on the Marquand Developments matter in a minute. So you'd better have a clear head."

I made a pig's ear of the document. After that, she seemed to take against me. I was relieved when her permanent secretary returned from extended sick leave, two days later. And the firm had no more work for me, so I left. As we say, 'The temp goes when the wind blows'.

I didn't think about the business over the pub until one day three months later, when Marcie phoned. She was going to be passing through on her way to the South Coast with her carload of children at lunchtime, and she suggested we meet up. It was a sunny day, and a picture of the beer garden came into my head.

"It's just the place on a day like this," I said. "Very child friendly. It's got a beer garden they can run around in, there's even a wishing well."

I got there late, and Marcie's loaded Estate was already in the little carpark. And I stumbled on her unexpectedly inside the gloomy bar, while my eyes were still getting accustomed to the change from the sunlight outside. She had Sarah, one of the five year olds, on her knee, in tears.

"What's up, Sarah?" I asked. She pouted. I turned to Marcie. "Why aren't you sitting outside?" She nodded down at the child for the answer.

"Mummy won't let me wish for my Winnie the Pooh. She says they've blocked the wishy well."

I tried to make a question mark with my face in Marcie's direction.

"Leslie, next time you suggest a lunch spot, do your homework. You've no idea the grief you've caused me."

"What's wrong with this? What's the problem with the wishing well?"

"Apparently, the District Council have made them cordon it off … for health and safety reasons!"

Marco came over, bearing menus. He looked awful, thin, much more like his cousin.

"I can't apologise enough Madam. I hope we can offer you lunch. We, we have a children's menu. You'd better not show it to the little girl though."
"No, I think we'd better leave. I'm sorry, but I don't think she'll stop until we're away from here." Marcie went out with Sarah to call the other children, who had gone out to play in the beer garden, while I sat.

Marco looked at me from across the counter, as if from a distance, through hollow, sunken eyes. "Aren't you from that law firm? With that solicitor who's in bed with Alistair?"

"Not any more. I was just a temporary secretary

there."

"You were here with them that day. You really stitched me up, you did. Why didn't you warn me the well couldn't be open? You knew, didn't you! All summer it's been boarded up. It was my USP, the wishing well, the beer garden, the swings. I can't get the turnover up to £100k, let alone £250k, and next week I'll lose the pub to Alistair. He won't give me more time to turn it around. 'That's the deal,' is all he says. And what does he gain? An empty loss-making pub without a manager. What's that good for?"

In the natural pause created by his rhetorical question, I reflected on the duty of confidentiality I owed to my ex-employer. But Amanda had said herself this issue fell outside the work she was doing.

"A loss-making pub is good if you're applying to the Planning Department for a change of use to residential."

"What do you mean?" He came out from behind the bar, and stood up against me, leaning over me. "That's lawyer's talk. What does it mean?"

"I'm not a lawyer," I said. "You don't need to be a lawyer to know a building like this is worth much more as a residential dwelling than as a pub. You could convert this into two, three nice flats."

"Alistair would just have bought it and converted it, if that had been his plan. He wouldn't have involved me." Doubt crept into his face. "It was him who contacted me, I didn't ask to get involved." I could see he was trying to reassure himself. "It was after I did the catering at my little sister's wedding, and he was there, and we got talking, and somehow I said I'd always fancied running a pub, and he said that was a coincidence, he was just looking to invest in a pub."

I wish I had left the conversation there. I expect the penny would have dropped sooner or later, even if I had, but it might not have come as such a blow. As it was, I couldn't resist, maybe because I felt Amanda should have told him three months sooner.

"The Planning Department won't just let you buy a pub and convert it to housing. You have to prove it's not viable as a pub first."

I have often wondered what 'thunderstruck' meant, and why they don't say 'lightning-struck'. Now I saw. It was as if the weight of the sounds – quiet speech, not rolling thunder – had struck him a heavy blow across the back.

Marco tottered.

"You mean … he never wanted the business to succeed?"

His features darkened. An unhealthy purple crept up his face, and the veins stood out at his neck and his temple. He paused, recollecting, calculating.

"But he let me spend his money on it." Another pause. "Not enough though. Not enough. I kept telling them. He wouldn't invest enough to make it work."

He fell back into a chair, as if he was exhausted.

"I kept asking the solicitor woman if it was normal. I couldn't understand it – invest a bit now, see if it attracts customers, and invest more if it does. It never made sense. But she just kept saying she couldn't comment, it was commercial." He looked up at me. "You worked there. Did she know?"

I said nothing. What could I say? That I needed Amanda's consent to disclose? That I would have to phone the temp agency, and get them to ask the firm?

He raised himself with an effort, and stumbled over

to me. "Did she know?" he repeated, into my face. I said nothing. He actually grabbed me by the lapels, lifted me bodily, and shook me, seething, spitting the words into my face "Did she know?"

As I was lifted, I felt abnormally calm, passive: somehow I knew that his violence was not directed at me and that I did not need to fight or fly. I remembered reading that when David Livingstone was mauled by a lion, he felt this abnormal calm. I was so calm that the words ran through my head 'Unhand me, knave' and yet I had the further presence of mind not to say them.

He threw me back into my chair.

"That Alistair, he knew muggins here would show how to lose money running a pub." He sank down again into the chair himself.

We both sat in silence. I think he was sobbing.

Then he stood up, with energy. "We made a wish at the wishing well. Together. I know it sounds stupid for two grown men. I just assumed we both wished for the pub to be a success. But his wish was for me to fail. I'll show him," he raised his voice, "I'll make sure nobody buys his flats," and he bolted into the beer garden, slamming the heavy door behind him.

I sighed with relief. I jumped as the door opened, quietly this time. Thankfully, it was Marcie. "What's wrong with the man who served us? He's really having a go at the boarding at the bottom of that garden."

I heard banging and ripping sounds from outside.

"I'll just use the bathroom," she continued, and then we'd better find somewhere else to eat. Hold on to Sarah, will you?"

I tried to comfort the little girl. "Do you want a Winnie

the Pooh then? Maybe we can find a Winnie the Pooh shop for you."

"I don't want a shop one. I want a real wishy one."

The heavy door opened again. It was Nicholas, beaming.

"Hi Uncle Leslie," he said, and turned to Sarah, "Come on, you can make your wish now. The man's uncovered the wishing well. And it really is magic, because he disappeared."

I followed the children outside. Marco had vanished. We went over to the well, and I held Sarah's hand as she leaned over and threw her penny in. Then I peered down into it. The cross-bars over it had been removed, as part of the work on it.

"Careful Uncle Leslie," shrieked Nicholas, "you might disappear too."

"What do you mean, 'too'?"

"I told you, the man disappeared."

"You mean he disappeared down the well? Very funny; he wouldn't fit."

"He did." Nicholas sounded earnest.

It was deep, black, the ferns growing in the walls near the top gave way to darker moss and then blackness. In the silence, I heard an echo coming from the depths. Was that a groan?

"Someone call 999", I heard myself shout.

Even when I left, the Fire Brigade were still trying to retrieve the body. It kept getting jammed as they tried to pull it up. An ambulance waited in the car park, next to the fire engines and police cars. It had been necessary to demolish the structure on the wishing well, the roof and winch, to set up their own winching equipment. A white tent had been erected over it all.

That night, I could not sleep. Every time I dozed off, I was falling into a black hole, getting stuck and being yanked out by my feet. Then Marco was in love with Amanda and Amanda was in love with Alistair, and now Amanda was getting married to Alistair beside the well and she was telling Marco she had never loved him and that he owed it to her to throw himself down the well for her sake.

The following week I went to the funeral. I thought it might help. Amanda was there in a figure-hugging black wool dress, but looking haggard, her skin waxy and over-made up. Alistair was sitting on the other side of the pews, with the family, looking relaxed in one of the same dark suits he wore every day.

I watched Amanda as the service went on. She was composed now, her face like alabaster. Until the priest started his funeral oration:

"No man can serve two masters: for either he will hate the one and love the other; or else he will hold to the one, and despise the other. Ye cannot serve God and mammon." The priest paused. "Matthew 6:24. And Marco Grouse," the priest continued, "was one who chose God above mammon ..."

But I did not hear what he said next. I was distracted by movement in the pews. Someone was leaving. Amanda. The alabaster had cracked, tears were streaming down her face and she was fleeing, fumbling along the pew as if blind. As if the priest's words were a scourge chasing her out of the temple. The side door crashed behind her.

I looked over at Alistair. He had not moved. He seemed deep in thought. At prayer? Or making his next wish.

The Black Hole

Leslie inwardly frowned. They shouldn't be asking him, who had read the 1805 *Prelude* three times from cover to cover, to spend a week listing someone's files. He checked himself. Shouldn't they? What had the growth of a poet's mind to do with anything here, in this glass and steel office in the West End? He had agreed to sell his mind during office hours, and there were no bidders at the moment other than James Brown & Brown Solicitors at £20 per hour. And he particularly needed the money: he was being evicted from his low-rent flat, and he had to find and pay for another which was bound to be a lot more expensive.

"Will that be okay?" asked Clifton, peering at him from behind an enormous desk on which there were numerous neat stacks of paper, evenly spaced, like an unimaginative development of low-rise office blocks.

"Thank you," said Leslie, unable to add a smile.

"I thought for a moment you had a problem with it."

"No. You want me to do that for the whole week, you say? It will be … a pleasure, a … holiday."

"If it was a holiday, I wouldn't be giving it to you."

Leslie followed Clifton's eyes, as he switched his gaze from Leslie to the glass partitioning and beyond towards

Marjorie Pryle, who was draped provocatively across her desk in conversation with a young tieless man, sub-clerical. The young man must have had a watchful eye, because when Clifton swept his arm in his direction, as if swatting away a fly, he jumped up and buzzed off. Clifton looked pleased. He did not smile. He never did: a warthog rather than a crocodile, roughly sixty, rotund but carried his weight lightly when he walked, his steel-heeled shoes clacking briskly along the corridors. It was inconceivable that the curvaceous young woman beyond the partition would return the interest he showed in her, other than at the minimal level required to keep her job. She met that level momentarily now, by dipping her cleavage in his direction.

Clifton turned back to him. "Don't you want to know where you are to list files? Whose files you are to list?"

"Very much," said Leslie.

"In the Black Hole, Jacklin's office." He paused dramatically, as if awaiting a pantomime gasp of horror. It did not materialise, because Leslie had no idea what he was talking about. "Do you know why we call Jacklin's office the Black Hole?"

"Because all matter is absorbed into a singular region of infinite density?"

"In a manner of speaking, yes. A lot less always seems to come out of his office than goes in. And yet the room is exceedingly neat. Jacklin specialises in Wills and Probate, and in that line of work they usually accumulate papers. But not him. Letters, files, bundles of paper all go in; what does he do with them, where do they go? He's been with us ten years now, so his room should gradually have piled up; the pile should reach the ceiling by now. But it doesn't." He looked down at the neat paper piles over his own desk. "Nothing even on his desk."

"A clear desk is a suspicious desk," interjected Leslie, "is that what you're saying? The perils of a 'clear desk' policy! One firm I worked at, there was a solicitor there whose desk was always clear, Adam Widnes. The drawers were crammed so full that the desk had to be broken up to open them. And then they found a letter: it would have saved a lot of trouble if that letter had been answered, instead of tucking itself away in that drawer."

"He does his own filing, and that makes me nervous. I'm on notice that no-one looks at his files, not even a secretary. I can't let that happen, as managing partner. I'd like a list of his files, open and closed. And I'd like you to take a look in each file."

"What am I to look for? Macavity?"

Clifton ignored him. "I want you to check that every time something comes in on a file, something goes back out. I want you to tell me when something's not there."

"Exactly. *For when a crime's discovered, then Macavity's not there!*"

"Mmm. Depending on what you find, I'll get someone with some qualifications to have a proper look."

Qualifications! exclaimed Leslie to himself, when he was out of the room. Looking for what was not there was his specialism.

Five minutes later, Leslie was staring at the engraved nameplate on Jacklin's door. "Rupert Jacklin, Partner", screwed onto the door with the permanence of a brass plaque screwed onto a coffin lid. He gazed momentarily through the porthole: reconnaissance. He saw a great big man on an even bigger chair, sitting behind a great big desk, staring at a single sheet of paper before him. Nothing on the wide flat plain at all other than a computer screen and a wireless mouse and keyboard. No intray, no knick knacks, not even a stapler. Closed filing cabinets. No stray papers or piles of files either on the floor or on any other surface. He must have a Napoleon of a secretary to organise him that well, Leslie thought, until he remembered Clifton said he did his own filing. There was something suspicious about that level of tidiness. How rigid, how … tight-arsed, must he be.

"Enter," boomed Jacklin, waving a welcoming paw. He had caught Leslie staring, but he was unperturbed. He was one of those men who permanently look as if they have just got out of a very hot bath, the pink skin glowing even to the roots of the thin white hair on the head. The circulation of blood at the surface was free, but what clogging of the arteries below? The slack physique betrayed that no exercise preceded the baths he took. Shirt as clean and crisp as the man's skin. Bold pin-striped trousers, jacket over chair. Superficially in shape, then.

Jacklin had no idea who Leslie was, or what he had been asked to do.

"I'm the temp."

"What do you mean, the temp? The temporary? Temporary what?"

"The temporary secretary."

For an instant the pink skin flared purple. Momentarily, that look of disdain, so familiar to Leslie, entered the eyes. And then he recovered himself and spoke.

"But I don't need a secretary when Jackie's away. Carla can manage my typing on top of Johnson's."

"I've been asked by Mr Clifton to make a list of your files."

"He gets the printout of all my files every month. The truth is that you've been sent to check up on me. They think I may be hiding problems in my filing cabinet, so they've sent you to have a snoop. But that's not your fault. Help yourself! Be my guest!"

Not a shadow crossed his face. As closely as Leslie looked, he could not see in Jacklin's eyes that almost invisible film descend, the lizard eyed glaze of someone trying to look unperturbed. A touch of defensiveness would be normal, thought Leslie. Most would bristle. After all, it is as close as you can get to inspecting a lawyer's mind, to read his files.

No, Jacklin was helpfulness itself. And if the contents of his filing cabinets were a reflection of his mind, then his mind must be as neat as a piano keyboard, thought Leslie. Listing the files was one of the easiest jobs he had ever been given. It was therefore exceedingly boring, and he was glad Clifton had asked him to take a look in each file. He opened file no. 23543, 're. the estate of Andrew Cutling'. Old Mr Cutling, who he saw from the death certificate had been a company director, was attempting to continue to direct from beyond the grave, to impose his will even after he was dead. Why did he care what would happen to his worldly goods? Mary Cutling, wife; Terence and Theresa, children; Martha Carnaby: who was she? Company secretary? Inheriting a town house?

"You're looking at the Cutling file are you?" It was Jacklin. "Hell hath no fury, and all that. Mary Cutling is trying to stop the girlfriend getting the house."

"And can she?"

"No. But she's the executor, so she can make things difficult. As she did for Mr Cutling while he was alive; he couldn't die quickly enough, to get some peace." He paused. "You're not just a temporary secretary then, you're some sort of file auditor, are you?" Leslie detected the slightest note of concern.

"No, I really am just a temp."

"No offence, but one doesn't see many male secretaries." Leslie could tell Jacklin's sense that he was a threat had evaporated. He had returned to being a nothing in Jacklin's eyes, in the eyes of the world. And why was he a nothing, why was he listing files at the age of thirty-five? How had he missed the bus? The answer rose like a chorus in his head: his Great Novel. His name had even been listed in an article about the twenty-five Emerging Writers to Watch. But the message from the agents and the publishers was consistent, however many times he rewrote it: his particular Great Novel was 'before its time'. After it, the Commercial Novel had been rejected in turn as 'uncommercial, it needs a stronger hook.' For his writing he had taught himself to touch-type, and to support his writing habit he had taken to verbal prostitution, selling himself, his fingers at least and the lower parts of his brain (leaving the upper part of the brain intact for his art) as a secretary.

Leslie was jolted out of his reverie. He had got a feel for the file numbering, and the file in his hand was an early one. Five years old. And yet it had acquired no bulk. A single cardboard folder, light as the coffin of a dessicated maiden aunt. If nothing had come of it, shouldn't the file have been closed? He opened it. Just a dozen sheets. Jacklin's initial letter dated 23rd October 2007, the four page client engagement letter, was there, promising to deliver the high quality of service on which the firm prided itself. There was a series of five short handwritten letters on cream lined paper in a spidery copybook hand, correspondence from some elderly relative of the deceased, the executor presumably. The handwriting deteriorated a little each year, classic copybook at first but shaking progressively more towards the spidery. As the years went by the language, instead of becoming more insistent, became more diffident, until the final letter, written only one week ago, said:

Dear Mr Jacklin

I refer to your last letter dated 15th January inst. It is appreciated that the weighty demands of your responsibilities must leave little room for a routine matter such as this, and I await hearing from you at your convenience.
Thank you for inquiring after Crufty. His hind leg has ever since been stiff, but we hobble off for walks quite nicely together.
If Victor's medals are found, I would appreciate being given the opportunity to purchase them.

Yours sincerely
Marion England

As with all the previous letters, Jacklin had responded on the very day he had received it:

Dear Marion

The administration of the estate is receiving my attention and will be addressed in due course. I am glad to hear that Crufty is back on all four paws. The hunt for Victor's medals continues.

Yours sincerely
Rupert Jacklin

The only other items in this thinnest of files were a copy of the will, leaving everything to the Cats Protection League, the death certificate giving the cause of death as pneumonia and advanced senile dementia, and a receipt from a house clearance firm listing contents cleared and sold, including a boxed Distinguished Flying Cross sold for £150.00.

Jacklin had lied: the medal had been sold. And the administration of the estate was not receiving his attention. He had taken no steps at all for over five years.

Jacklin was out of the room. Leslie looked at his watch: lunchtime. He placed the file on the clear desk, and went out. He was back before Jacklin, and when he eventually returned, his complexion was ruddier, but the freshness of the morning had been dulled by wine.

"What's this file doing here?"

Leslie searched his face for a sign of guilt: for reddening of the cheeks, or whitening of the lips, for a sigh released or a gulp swallowed. Nothing. "I thought you might want to …"

Jacklin pushed the file away from him. "I don't suppose I can save it forever. In due course … But be a dear fellow, and put it back for the moment, will you, and pass me down the Shiftwater file, just the latest correspondence file." Then he looked up at Leslie.

"Don't look so worried. What's there to worry about? It's in the black hole, old boy." He laughed to himself.

"The black hole! You wouldn't understand, you need to know the law. Trust me.

"It can wait. Victor England's house stands empty, weatherproof, it won't fall down, and it's in Wimbledon so its value can only go up. His money is safe in the bank, where it gleams silently, industriously at work. Interest accumulates. The shares go up and down on their own, no need to pull strings. As with the money, the dividends accumulate. The clock doesn't even start ticking until I apply for Probate, and that's when the charity will find out about the gift: it's a windfall for them, they'll be delighted.

"I know what you're thinking. They may not be delighted, they would have liked their money sooner ... that's when you need to know the law. They can't touch me! You see the beneficiary – the cat charity, isn't it – may have suffered a loss, but the law says I owe no duties to them. I owe my duties to the executor, Miss England, but she hasn't suffered a loss because the estate doesn't go to her. So she could sue, but she hasn't suffered a loss. The cats have suffered a loss, but they can't sue. A black hole, where there's no remedy. It's a marvellous thing sometimes, the law!

"Hmmm," hummed Leslie, "so the cats must wait and go hungry."

"Hunger? What do you know of hunger? You're not a professional man, you don't know the fear of famine, the professional's fear that he will run out of work. I have these cases" – he waved his arm across his filing cabinets – "but I've squeezed what I can out of most of them. Why should anyone else ever instruct me? And if they don't, how do I pay the school fees? How do I eat? No, I keep the England file up my sleeve, in the larder, along with the other silent ones, for the day when I would otherwise go hungry.

"These files," he waved his hand at a row of fat ones, bulging with correspondence, "these are the greedy geese. Take the Paget estate here: Mrs Paget's five children, all in their fifties, had been willing her to die for years so they could pay off their mortgages, eyeing the furniture and rushing home to check the value of each piece on the internet. And now she's dead, they're at each other's throats because the youngest girl – I say girl but even she's in her early fifties, recently divorced – got her to do a new will a week before she died, leaving everything to her. They're on the phone every day, and the estate is being eaten up in my fees. What would I do if I ran out of greedy relatives? That's when I'll deal with the England file. I keep it for a rainy day. The cats don't even know what they've inherited, and Miss England is in no hurry. She's a dog lover; I don't think she even cares for cats."

Leslie shrugged, put the file back in the cabinet, and took out the next one.

But the file continued to prey on his mind. More specifically, the empty house. He could be living in it himself. He knew Wimbledon, and he could tell from the address that it would be what estate agents call a detached villa, highly desirable. He wouldn't be able to afford the rent on a place like that in his wildest dreams. It would be £4,000 a month or more: £50,000 a year!

He scratched his head. £50,000 a year, the cats were missing out on. Five years had passed, so £50,000 x 5. £250,000. Just so that Jacklin had some work in hand for a rainy day. Jacklin should have let out the house, but of course he would have had to apply for probate to do that, and that would start the clock running. Those cats would be cross if they knew! But Jacklin was saying they couldn't complain about anything he did or didn't do. And Miss England, the dog lover, she could complain but the £250,000 wasn't money that would be hers? So Jacklin could lose the estate £250,000 and no-one would have any remedy against him? Was the law really that much of an ass?

Leslie looked up from the file he was meant to be checking. Jacklin had his head down, making notes down the side of the single page on his desk, with a gold propelling pencil.

"Wouldn't a judge," said Leslie, breaking the silence, "wouldn't a judge say that for the time being, Miss England is the owner of her brother's property? So she has suffered a loss after all, when the property should have been let out for the last five years, isn't that what a judge would say?"

Jacklin reddened, a deep tomato red, different now from the fresh red of the morning or the post-prandial glow. *Leslie had crossed a line. It was a comment which Jacklin might have accepted from an equal. Professionals don't like being told what to do.*

"Let out for the last five years?" he imitated, putting on a thin, weak, sarcastic voice. "Wouldn't a judge say?"

Now his voice lowered, to a booming explosion. "Who do you think you are? I'm not going to be told my job by a secretary, a male secretary at that. Do you have a legal qualification? Did you spend three years at Cambridge? The professional exams? Twenty years of experience in practice? Perhaps you would like to sit behind my desk and give me dictation, would you? Do you know why you are a secretary and I am a solicitor?"

"I know why I'm a secretary. I did spend three years at Cambridge actually. I did English. Unlike most of my friends, who slid more or less painlessly down the slide from Arts degrees into the mincing machine of law school, I was stupid enough to try to spend ten years trying to write a novel. In the course of typing out all 100,000 words three times, although the third draft was probably shorter than the first, I acquired exceptional typing skills. And in order to capture the language of living men, as Wordsworth put it, I taught myself shorthand, which I have never once used as a secretary."

"Yes, well, it's reassuring to have a Cambridge-educated secretary, but until you get the legal qualifications, I suggest you confine your concerns to the literary."

Leslie was spending his evenings looking at new flats to rent in south-west London, and when he found himself in the locality of Victor England's vacant house, he could not resist going to have a look. It was on a busy street, but set back and dark, hidden by trees and shrubs from the orange glow of street lights. When he went through the shrubs to the windows it felt silent and secret, and he felt like a burglar. There was nothing to see through the windows: the house had been stripped bare, even the curtains gone. For an instant he saw himself breaking in, unlocking the door from the inside, moving in his belongings, living there; camping: he would be without electricity, but he could have a gas stove, gas lights. The instant passed. He returned to the road, and waited at the bus-stop.

Car brakes screeched. A small dark bundle tumbled

along the road, and came to a stop in the gutter. But then it came to life, a black cat, its body snapping open and shut like a folding knife, back and forth, shrieking. Suddenly, the movement and shrieking stop, and it lay silent. The assembled queue stared in horror, paralysed, until a slight young woman went over, threw her coat over it, bundled it tight in the coat, picked it up in her arms, hailed a taxi, and drove away.

"If only there was an animal ambulance," said a voice in the crowd.

It was a sign. If you sold that house, you could have a helicopter, an animal air ambulance. The rent alone it could have earned would have paid for a fleet of ambulances.

The next evening, the Thursday, Leslie found a new flat. It was expensive, and it was small, very small: living room and kitchen, bathroom, bedroom. If he had C around, svelte as she was they would spend their time bumping into one another; it would be an intimate experience, and that decided him to take it.

Now it was Friday. He had found nothing else in his trawl of Jacklin's files. There were a couple of other cases where there was no greedy relative to chivvy Jacklin along, but the cases were meandering rather than stagnant. Lunchtime came, and his week was up.

"It's been a pleasure to have your company," said Jacklin. "Is there anything you want to check with me before you speak to Clifton?" he said it in an artificially relaxed tone, as if he was offering to do him a favour. His eyes, as well as his voice, gave him away.

Clifton took the list from him, but he did not read it. He

did not even flick through it. "Is there a client engagement letter on every file?"

"Yesss…" Leslie drawled as if inserting a "but". Clifton did not take the bait. He had already ticked the box.

"Does he answer letters, calls, emails, promptly?"

"Yesss…" Again, Leslie filled his voice with diffidence. Every letter was answered on the England file; that was not the problem.

"Are there any letters of complaint?"

"No." How could there be a complaint on the England file, when Jacklin had Miss England in the palm of his hands?

"Very good. That's all I need."

"There was one file I wondered about," started Leslie, tentatively.

"What, a complaint on it?"

"No. It wasn't …" Clifton cut him off.

"Unanswered letters? No client engagement letter?"

"No."

"Exercise done then. I wouldn't expect a secretary to be competent to opine on the quality of a partner's work. Even Jacklin's." The look in Clifton's eyes told Leslie that he thought him incapable of anything more than a mechanical exercise.

Leslie started seeing cats everywhere. Outside the flat he now had one week left to inhabit, he saw an emaciated cat look on while dustmen emptied overflowing compost bins. A late night documentary about cats kept prisoner in high rise buildings, which never went outside except onto a balcony, declawed so that they did not ruin the furniture. When he took a load of junk from the flat to the recycling centre, he saw newborn kittens in a cardboard box.

He needed the address. Miss England's address. It would be in the firm's database: access denied. Or in the Word documents on the server: access denied. He would have to get it the old-fashioned way. The following lunchtime, he poked his head into Jacklin's office. He was out. Leslie's heart thumped; he was a spy in the Nazi headquarters. They would hang him with piano wire if he was caught. He walked straight over to the cabinet, pulled the file out, and opened it.

Aarggh. Jacklin walked in. Panic was engulfing him, until Jacklin sat down at his desk, as if Leslie was not there. The cloak of invisibility that you assumed as a secretary, like a servant picking up the clothing of his master and mistress as they lay oblivious in bed. Leslie looked at the address: he could not write it down, but he fixed the address in Slough in his mind, and the postcode was easy to remember: SL1 1MY, like a corny personalised numberplate. He moved towards the door.

"Got what you need?" asked Jacklin absentmindedly as he left.

Saturday was the day he moved into his new compact flat. The process of compacting his furniture into the reduced space exhausted him, and by the evening he was ready to abandon his plan. But when he woke up on Sunday and surveyed the piles of unopened boxes that filled the room, the idea of a day out struck him as attractive. He found his suit folded in a box. He found the ironing board, against a wall behind a stack of boxes, but he could not find the iron, so he put on his shirt crumpled as it was.

The address was a small semi-detached on a busy road, much inferior to the house in Wimbledon. The paint was beginning to peel on the front door. When he rang the bell there was a scraping behind the door, and a bark. "Quiet, Crufty," he heard in an old lady's voice, as the door opened. "Can I help you?"

"Miss England?" She nodded. "I've come about your brother."

A look of horror passed across her face. Then it was gone, but she was visibly shaken. "I have to sit down," she said. "Come on through. Don't mind Crufty, he won't bite."

He followed her, muttering "You shouldn't really be letting in strangers," but she did not seem to have heard. Perhaps it was his suit that reassured her.

She led him into the time-warped sitting room; heavy furniture, armchairs and a sofa with antimacassars, and clocks, there were at least four clocks ticking loudly. No TV. Once she was seated, not in an armchair but stiffly upright in a reproduction Chippendale, she spoke.

"I used to dread that," she looked towards the front door, "in the War. They'd send a man from the Ministry like you to deliver the bad news. And what with Vic being a pilot, we dreaded every knock on the door." She paused.

"But I don't have anything to dread now. He's done his worst. What did you say you'd come about?"

"It's about Victor's will."

"Oh that. He always had a sense of humour, and he did it to spite me, leaving it all to those cats. And leaving his own sister to live like this." She looked around her, as if surveying a rubbish tip instead of a respectable, if old fashioned, living room.

"I thought you might be a cat-lover, like your brother," said Leslie, to break the silence.

"Crufty doesn't like cats, and nor do I," she replied. "My brother did though. He was for cats, and I was for dogs; cat and dog, we fought over that all our lives, ever since we were children. Our parents, they wouldn't have either, said animals were just another mouth to feed, unless they were working for their keep."

"He liked cats. So that was why he left his money …"

"He wanted the last laugh. The coward, didn't tell me to my face, left me thinking it was all coming to me. The only thing I want now is his silly medal, so I can burn it. He was a bully as a boy, and he's still bullying me. I'm in no hurry to sort out that will of his. It can wait forever as far as I'm concerned."

"Well," he started, "that was what I came to discuss."

After that visit, Leslie steered well clear of Jacklin's office. He had a near miss when he walked past Reception one day, and saw Miss England sitting with her stiffly upright posture in the waiting room, but he was confident that she did not see him.

It was over a month later, while he was washing his hands in the Gents, that he saw Jacklin approach in the mirror. Jacklin came to the basin next to him, turned on the tap and let it run.

"Funny thing", he said, without turning to Leslie, "on one of the files of mine you looked at. The England file, the one I was saving. It came to life. The old biddy said she'd had her collar felt by the CPL. They actually sent someone round to see her. I made discreet inquiries in that direction, because they couldn't have known about the will unless someone told them. What's really odd, is that they say no-one did tell them. They say they never knew anything about the legacy until I wrote to them. They say they have no record of sending anyone round to visit the old lady, and they say they never would. Any ideas?"

The tap was still running.

"I expect they're grateful to you for drawing it to their attention," said Leslie.

"Yes, they are grateful. So much so that they've sent me some instructions. I'm on their panel of solicitors. It's all splendid."

"And presumably there's no chance they'll complain about the delay. Which is a good thing after that judgment which I saw you had put in the file."

"Judgment?"

"You know," said Leslie. "That decision where the judge said, now let me get this right, he said," and he started speaking with great rapidity, as if reciting something memorised, which he was: "the executor of an estate is entitled to bring a claim for negligence against solicitors where the loss was suffered by a beneficiary of the will and not the executor himself as, during the time of the loss, the property was vested in the executor."

Leslie looked at Jacklin in the mirror. He had turned white, and he stuttered:

"The judgment's in the file, did you say?"

"It was there by the time I'd finished, I mean … when I reviewed the file."

The mirror was empty. Jacklin was gone, and the tap was still running. Leslie smiled to himself and turned it off.

Leslie left the firm shortly afterwards. The secretary whose absence he had been recruited to cover had long since returned, but Clifton's PA had taken to sending him an email every Friday afternoon, asking him to plug another gap the next week. It had been a longer run of serendipitous openings than usual. But one Friday, no email materialised. There is no notice period as a temp. On a Friday afternoon, silence is termination. They do not tell you they need you for the Monday, and you are gone. There is no pretence: there are no 'thank you's or 'Sorry You're Leaving' and then you turn the page to "This Dump won't smell the same without you!". You leave the island without saying your goodbyes. You keep in touch with no-one, because you were only ever temporary.

And you move on yourself. You never find out what happened next. You are not meant to be curious about what is going on in your absence in any office, because the essence of your job is that you do not belong.

So it came as a surprise to Leslie, while sipping his coffee one Saturday morning, and idly turning over the pages of the local paper on the wide table, to read:

Cat-lover dies in mercy swerve

Respected local solicitor and animal-lover Rupert Jacklin died from injuries sustained when he crashed his car, after he swerved to avoid a cat. He was certified dead at the scene. The vehicle, which police say was within the speedlimit, ran off the tree-lined road into a tree. Local councillors have criticised the Highway Authority for failing to remove the trees. A spokesman for the Cats Protection League praised Mr Jacklin's heroism, but stressed that drivers should not endanger themselves or other road-users for the sake of animals.

Cat lover! Well, Clifton would be glad of the list of files, he thought, and if God was a Cat (it seemed to Leslie much more likely that he was a Dog, given the shared letters) he would look less unfavourably on Jacklin than if he had continued to sit on that file.

Buttons and Diamonds

The other day, the managing partner sent an email round the office, telling us that we were no longer to use window envelopes. I didn't think anyone actually sent out hard copies these days. But apparently they do in the Family Department, and apparently a letter went out addressed to a client. The client was a woman who had decided to leave her husband, but had not yet broken the news to him. The letter was badly folded, with the result that the matter heading had been visible in the window: "re your proposed divorce". The proposed respondent husband happened to hear the clatter of the postbox and in an uncharacteristically helpful act in that stale marriage, he brought the letter to the stale breakfast table. As bad luck would have it, he had his reading glasses on.

Therein lies the peril of window envelopes. But the email reminded me of my sister's experience, which proved that non-window envelopes have perils too. I wanted to send the managing partner a reply to his email, but my recollection was hazy. So I phoned Carolina, in Australia. She is fine. Her husband is fine. Her second son has started at Sydney University, and her teenage daughter is playing up even worse than she did herself. Yes, she remembers it.

"How could I forget it," she adds. "It changed my life."

She has calmed down a lot in the twenty-five years since she went to live in the Outback. She went to Australia because somehow she had realised that the tall cluttered London buildings were a dead end for her, and so was the narrow social circle in which she drifted nightly from cocktail party to dinner to nightclub. She livened the gatherings, but the gatherings did not liven her. She had recognised a need in herself for the wide landscapes, the empty plains and even the empty evenings.

She only went to work in a law firm because she was saving for her plane ticket. I had told her that legal secretaries were paid more than secretaries elsewhere. She didn't have the legal training, but she picked it all up quickly enough, and by February 1986 she had been there almost a year.

Everyone was in a hurry that afternoon at Black & Pugh. There was snow. She has not seen it since, and she now remembers it as in a fairytale: big snowflakes flurrying across the window by her workstation, out of the dark snow-heavy clouds. Unusually for London, it was settling on the whitening pavement below. There was that silence which snow brings. It was a Friday, and everyone was in a quiet hurry, keen to get away early before they were snowed in at work for the weekend.

Mark Easton, the partner she worked for, always left early on a Friday, "to drive down to the country seat, don't you know", he would say, putting on a mock aristocratic accent. He brought her a tape. He always did at about 4.30pm.

"One more tape, my flower, a short one this time. Just a couple of letters. Then you're free, and you and your boyfriend can ... do your thing all weekend", he filled the gap with a subtle movement of his hips that shook his belly. Did he know she did not have a boyfriend? She blushed and said nothing.

She had spent the morning copy-typing a tremendously boring agreement, and then there had been amendments. Now he had brought her the tape. Usually when he said "a couple of letters" it turned out to be half a day's worth of work. But this time he was true to his word: on the new tape were just two short letters, gabbled off at speed, with not so much as a pause between them. The first was to his great catch. He had recently broken into the glamorous film industry, and he was acting for a number of film distributors. Now, he had received instructions to represent Cloud Films, the market leader. He had dictated:

To Cloud Films:

Dear Anthony
Re. your dispute with Storm Films
Thank you for sending me the distribution agreement, which I have reviewed. I am afraid clause 8 is, as Storm Films allege, ambiguous, and I will call you early next week to discuss ways to bring the dispute to an early resolution. In the meantime, I am telling their solicitors that the allegations will be vigorously disputed, because if we conceded at this crucial stage that you have no defence, they could apply for judgment, which would be disastrous.
Yours etc.

To Lisners, Solicitors:

Dear Sirs
Your client: Storm Films
Our client: Cloud Films
We have now had an opportunity to review the distribution agreement. Our clients dispute your client's allegations, and will vigorously defend your client's claims, in particular the claim that clause 8 is in any way ambiguous, which is denied.
Yours etc.

Before she had finished typing, she was aware of him standing over her in his coat, staring down her front. His breath was stale.

"I was coming to tell you," he said, "they can wait until Monday, but if they're done…". He always said that. He signed the first as she tore the second one out of her machine. He signed the second, and he was gone.

"Bloody typical," moaned Stacey from the workstation next to her, "they're paid five times what we are, but they're out the door at the first f-ing snowflake."

Carolina hummed agreement, as she fed an envelope into the typewriter. She was not looking forward to her journey home. The train would be crowded and late. She had gone back to her mother's to live, to save money, but her mother lived in the Greenbelt. During the week, she lived a nomadic life, staying in London, camping on the floors of friends. Her saving scheme was not getting anywhere: either there was the train fare to Twyford, or the expensive evenings out in London. She looked at her watch. Damn. She put the letters in the envelopes, grabbed her coat, and swept down the stairs where Frank had already turned off the franking machine.

"Room for two more little ones?" she begged in the little girl voice which made even her cringe.

When she opened the door, and felt the icy blast of cold air, and entered the muffled world of white, she forgot her cringeworthy remark, she forgot typing and bosses, law firms and money. But she wished she was not wearing her pumps. Pulling her coat around her, she slipped and slid along towards the Underground.

By Monday morning, the snow was starting to thaw, but it still took her three hours to get into work, and Mark was not even there. He came in after lunch, looking awfully relaxed. By Tuesday, everything was back to normal, the snow had melted and whiteness had given way to London's bitter greys and blacks.

It was back to normal outside. Instead, in the office Carolina sensed something had changed, as though an invisible blanket of snow had fallen inside. When she took Mark his morning coffee, he was frozen in the act of putting down the telephone receiver, perfectly still, his arm holding it suspended in mid-air. He was staring beyond her, white-faced. Should she spill hot coffee on his hand, to bring him round? But he unfroze of his own accord. He did not thank her: but that was normal, he never did. He did not look at her: he did normally do that, looking her up and down. He got up and almost pushed her out of the room, closing the door behind her. Later, when she came by and looked through the glass partition, he had disappeared.

Half an hour later, she was called to the Boardroom. Was Mark in trouble, she wondered. Serve him right if he was.

As she opened the door to the Boardroom, Mark was sitting next to Lord Isaac at the far end of the mahogany table, under Lord Isaac's portrait. Mark was not in trouble then. Her entrance seemed to have interrupted them, and she asked should she go. But they pointed to a chair already pulled out. There was a glass of water there, on a coaster. She sat. Mark cleared his throat. He was speaking. Lord Isaac looked on. It was a serious matter, Mark was saying. It took her a few moments to tune in. She had done a bad thing. They were appalled.

"Your carelessness has cost me my best client … Cloud Films." He said the name with genuine grief in his voice, as if the company had been a living being that had died. "It is a very grave matter for the firm"

"A very grave matter indeed," echoed Lord Isaac in his soft, velvety voice.

"What are you saying?"

Mark did not stop. So serious that they had no option. But to ask her to leave the building. At once. At once, echoed Lord Isaac softly, at once. Black & Pugh could not tolerate such behaviour.

"What are you saying I have done?"

"I'm saying the firm can't tolerate such careless behaviour."

"What have I done that's careless?" She felt sick in her stomach.

"Don't act the innocent," there was iron behind the velvet in Lord Isaac's voice. "You sent the wrong letters to the wrong parties."

"Parties?" asked Carolina, confused, unable to grasp what they were saying. Mark stood up.

"You put my letter to Cloud Films in the envelope to Storm Films' lawyers, so Storm Films have applied for judgment, exhibiting the letter to their affidavit. Cloud Films have sacked us, and they have instructed Cordell & Co instead."

Lord Isaac took up the reins, the velvet in his voice regaining the upper hand. She would be paid to date of course, and any holiday entitlement would be paid in lieu. He slid an envelope down the long polished table, with an unexpected flick of the wrist. It floated silently along, into her hands.

"It's all in the letter," said Mark. As if that was a prearranged signal, he helped Lord Issac up, and they both left, closing the door behind them. She stared at the envelope, then opened it, but in her daze the words were meaningless.

Within what seemed moments, the door opened. Had it all been a mistake? No. Frank appeared with her coat over his arm and a banker's box of her things, including postcards that decorated the partition, her dead potplant and personal items taken from the bottom drawer of her desk. He looked worried, and he stumbled over his words as he told her he must accompany her – "ancompany", he said – out of the building. She walked past her cleared workstation, and past Stacey, who looked up momentarily at her as if she was seeing a ghost, and then looked back into her screen.

Frank was walking alongside her like a guard. Outside, he hailed a taxi, handed the cabbie a piece of paper and put her box in the front, before running back up the steps into the building. As she got in the open door, her legs suddenly gave way, and she collapsed into the seat. Her stomach turned over like the taxi's idling diesel engine. She could not tell what was shaking, the taxi or her.

"Where to, ma'am?"

"Victoria," she said without thinking.

She read the letter. Gross misconduct. Cloud Films had received the letter addressed to Storm Films. Storm Films were relying on the admissions in Mark's letter to Cloud Films. She had put them in the wrong envelopes. Copies of the two letters were enclosed. How could she have done it? They were right: she had been careless. Incompetent, the letter said. Yes. Amounting to recklessness. Yes, she could see that. She looked at the two letters again. She had been in too much of a rush to leave for her train.

Suddenly the taxi was at Victoria Station, but she did not move. A wave of self-pity overwhelmed her. She would never get away, never get to Australia. Tears welled in her eyes.

"You awright there, love?"

The taxi driver was looking at her in the mirror. She wiped her eyes and tried to smile.

"They've sacked you, haven't they, and stuck you in my cab. We call them funeral runs, we get a lot of them this time of day. You sit there long as you like." He waved Frank's piece of paper at her. "They're paying whatever's on the meter."

After a few moments he continued. "What you done wrong then? Give us a butcher's."

She handed him the letter. He read it in silence, then the other pages. Then read them again. He asked her careful questions, in a measured tone. Then he tossed the letter back.

"Worth about five grand, that."

"They're going to sue me?" she asked, alarmed.

"No love. You-are-going-" he emphasised each word separately "-to-sue-them. Unfair dismissal, innit, and all deeply embarrassing for Mark. He'll be lucky if he isn't taken to the cleaners by them clients. Call himself a solicitor! He could even be up before the old beaks in the Law Society."

"What?"

"Think about it. I was a courier before I did me legs in. If someone gives me two packets, and they both feel the same, say they're padded envelopes and they both feel like they've got buttons in, well it's no sweat. But if he says to me 'This packet contains buttons, but *that* packet contains diamon's,' then I do sweat and I don't mix them up for the life of me. But it's his job, it's the chump who gives them to me, he's the one who's got to tell me is they diamon's or buttons. An' if he didn't, well he should be man enough to admit it now."

Her face must have revealed her confusion, because he added "They can't sack you for posting what feels like a packet of buttons to the wrong address. If they was diamon's, he should bleeding well have told you so. He's the one who screwed it up, and now he's let you take the rap for him." He paused. "Yeah, he should have checked 'em, instead of celebrating poet's day early."

"Poet's day?"

"Piss off early, tomorrow's Saturday."

In spite of the nightmare, she smiled.

"Now," he turned off the meter, and handed her his clipboard and pen, which she took with bemusement, "you go home, and when you've had your dinner, you're going to sit down and write them a letter. This is what you're going to say." And he dictated a legal letter, which could have been written by Mark or any of the lawyers she did the typing for.

When he had finished, she thanked him, and he looked awkward; through his gnarled cheeks she thought she saw a blush.

"You'll get two letters," he shouted after as she climbed the station steps. "One will tell you to piss off, and the other will offer you peanuts. Then you tell them to piss off, and they make a real offer. That's the one to take. Keep your chin up."

She got to the top of the steps before she realised she didn't have his name or taxi number so she could thank him properly, but when she turned he and his taxi were already gone, mingled back into the anonymous sea of London cabs – driving in, setting down, picking up and driving out, like bees around some outlandish glass beehive.

She followed his advice, but expected nothing. She contacted a Temp agency to get more work, not a law firm this time. She had had enough of law firms. A letter arrived two days later from the firm. The Black & Pugh headed notepaper already looked unfamiliar. It was addressed "Dear Madam" as if she had never worked there, its tone glacial, a short rejection of her allegations, which would be vigorously defended, with a counterclaim for damages for breach of her contract of employment.

There was no second letter. When it did not arrive the next day, her confidence in the taxi driver deserted her. After all, he was a cabbie, not a lawyer. They had been Mark's letters, yes, but it was her job to see that they went into the right envelopes. What had the cabbie said? A package of diamonds. Maybe every solicitor's letter was a package of diamonds. Maybe she should have known that.

When the second letter came a day later, she felt ashamed that she had doubted the cabbie. She looked at the postmark on the envelope. They had both been sent the same day, but for some reason this one had been held up.

She scanned the guarded language. No admission. Compromise. Full and final settlement. Taking into account claims against her. Full and final settlement (again). Attached cheque.

You and I would have seen a cheque for £1,000, and we would have thought that it was their opening offer, and we would have sent it back with a counter-offer to settle for £6,000, with a view to extracting a final offer of £3,000.

But Carolina did not see a cheque at all. She saw a one-way ticket to Australia and her first month's rent while she found a job in the sun, and maybe the price of some summer clothes. She did not care to barter. She had what she wanted.

"So," she concluded, "what I thought was the most awful day of my life, when they marched me out of the building, turned out to be the best thing that ever happened to me."

Rather than sending an email to the managing partner, I went to see him, and told him my sister's story over a cup of coffee. Needless to say, the firm is still using window envelopes.

What judgment shall I dread?

"I'll pay you by the word, not the hour. What's your typing speed?"

That was Malcolm Macaw for you. He wanted a secretary who would type away all evening, but he knew I would be doing it on top of my daytime job. Would I be as productive at the end of the day as in the first eight hours? He evidently doubted it.

I thought it best to go in low. "60 words a minute."

"Then I'll pay you …" he took out his calculator and played with it for a moment. "I'll pay you … a ha'penny a word."

A penny every two words? I did the calculation: £18 for each hour's work, and here's him charging clients £350 an hour.

"It's all going to be Conveyancing, isn't it?"

"You know what we do. We do one thing, and we do it well." The modulation of his voice deepened to the velvet tones of an advertiser. "Macaw & Co, Residential Property Solicitors, helping people to buy and sell their homes. That's it. Not Divorce, Crime or Litigation. Just Property."

Residential Property is bitty typing, all forms and short

letters. I'd be lucky to average 20 words a minute over an hour. If that. And then I must factor in my particular value to him as a male secretary, in the circumstances of his unfortunate history. 2p a word, I thought. That would give me roughly £24 an hour, much more if there were long deeds to type.

"3p a word," I said.

"2p."

"Done. I'll keep a tally of my word counts."

"And I probably won't get round to checking them." He laughed through his teeth. *'I'll check all right,'* said the teeth. "Can you start now? Agnetha is three tapes in arrears."

"You shouldn't have chosen your daytime secretary on looks alone. Then you wouldn't need a Rumpelstiltskin at night."

He blushed. As well he might.

I was to work evenings now and then, when there was a backlog. Malcolm already knew me. I'd worked for the firm before, and he was the sort of person who collected people as he came across them. I didn't feel an overwhelming compulsion to tell the agency, who would have wanted their cut. This was in my own time. And I was not doing it for fun. £1,000 was what I needed. £800 would get my car back on the road, and £200 might get my clarinet fixed. I had an estimate for the car, but not for the clarinet. 50,000 words. 42 hours.

Over the following month, I came in at least two evenings a week. It was peaceful. The office was empty and silent, like a ghost ship. It seemed a waste to have the lighting for a team of twenty blazing away throughout the office, when there was only Malcolm and me working. But apparently there was only one light switch for the whole central arena in which I was working, a sort of square goldfish bowl in which the secretaries and clerical staff swam around all day. The individual rooms for solicitors lined the edge of the central arena with glass windows, so the solicitors could watch how hard the staff were swimming. Each of those rooms had its own light, and they were all blacked out save for Malcolm's. In the evening, I like to work in the soft cocoon of a desklamp's glow. But when I asked, Malcolm said he liked looking into the glare, apparently it made him feel awake, alive.

"Anyway," he added, "the cleaner needs the lights on."

It was true. She arrived every evening to break the silence with the clatter of cleaning and the roar of her hoover. She was young, younger than me anyway, petite and energetic, although I noticed, as I watched her from the other side of the room, that her movements were stilted, as if she was clockwork. High-cheeked, Slavic looks. As I did every evening when she came to empty my bin, I tried to get her to talk, to break the monotony. She would never engage. I felt we should be fellow spirits: after all, we were both self-employed casual workers, she on zero hours, me on zero words. But perhaps her English was poor.

One evening, I was watching as she dipped down to empty the bins at the other side of the open plan area. I noticed that she turned her whole body. She did not twist her neck. She kept her back rigid. That was why her movements were stilted! So when she reached my bin I said:

"Is your neck troubling you?"

She stood up straight and rubbed the nape for a

moment, under her hair.

"Thank you, but I'm fine." She shrugged her shoulders when she spoke, as if shrugging me off, and moved on to the next bin at the next workstation.

I did no more than nod politely to her the following night. I did not want the sort of unfortunate experience that Malcolm had gone through. But to my surprise she stopped at my desk. Something had caught her eye. She pointed at my book. I was reading 'The Good Soldier' by Ford Maddox Ford, and it was on my desk.

She smiled. "Shvike?" she asked.

I guessed at her question. "Yes, I like it a lot," I said tentatively. She held out her hand, and I passed her the book. She looked inside the front cover. Her face fell, she shook her head and passed the book back to me.

"Not shvike," she said. She bent down stiffly for my bin, emptied it and moved on.

Shvike, shvike, shvike. What did she mean? I googled it. Nothing. I needed someone who spoke ... which Eastern European language exactly? I didn't even know which country she came from. It would sound ignorant to ask her.

In the end I didn't need to ask anyone, because it came to me in the night. Schvike. Schwike. Schweik. Schwejk. Švejk. Not 'The Good Soldier' by Ford Maddox Ford, but 'The Good Soldier Švejk', by Jaroslav Hašek. She must be Czech.

I was doing a couple of hours for Malcolm the following night, so I took in my copy, and put it on my desk.

Sure enough, "Švejk!" she said with glee, grabbed the book and held it to her breast like a love letter. "I did my PhD on Hašek."

"Where?" I asked.

"Charles University," she answered, as if I should know what that was. I scribbled down the name. Then she added: "But your copy is so ... crumpled, is that the expression?"

"It fell into the bath," I started to explain, but she would not let me.

"Hašek would like that, yes? I love Josef Švejk, I love the way he plays the idiot." She wiped away her smile. "I must do my work." She handed the book back to me. "But thank you for bringing it in."

And so she unfroze. But her neck didn't, and the following night, I asked her about it.

"The neck's not good," she said.

Everyone loves their own ailments, and I thought she would go on, but she needed a push.

"It's been bothering you for a while?"

"Sure." She did not continue. She turned to go. How could I engage her?

"How did you do it? I mean, how did you injure your neck?"

She was silent.

"Were you playing sport?" She looked sporty.

She remained silent, watching me.

"Or was it a car accident? Whiplash."

She nodded.

"Did you crash into them, or did they crash into you."

"They said we crashed into them. My boyfriend was driving."

My heart sank at the mention of a boyfriend, but I rallied. "You were the passenger, then?" I paused. "Are you still with that boyfriend?"

She went red, as if I had propositioned her.

"What is it to you?"

I blushed in my turn. I tried to smile away the awkwardness. "I only mean that if you were the passenger, it doesn't matter who's fault the accident was. So long as you don't mind suing your boyfriend. It won't affect him, just his insurers. You ought to be making a claim. For compensation."

"Yes, Mr Macaw already found a solicitor for me, and made me call them." So another white knight had got there before me.

Thump, step. Thump, step. The white knight himself. Malcolm's head appeared round the corner.

"Leslie, where's that lease? Hi Vessey. How's the neck?" But his head disappeared again before she could get out an answer, and he thump-stepped his way back to his desk. So her name was Vessey.

Vessey's serious face had brightened into a smile.

"He looks so funny with that plastercast on his ankle," she said, "when he's all dressed up in a gentleman's suit."

"I think he broke his ankle skiing," I started to say, but she had already reached down for my bin, and was gone.

The next evening, Vessey came straight up to me, and took an envelope out of her apron.

"They're saying I need you to witness my signature."

"Me?" Why me, I thought, suddenly feeling flattered, connected to Vessey.

"Not you. Someone. Anyone. I need to sign my name and you sign yours underneath. See, it says in the letter here."

I scanned the letter. Datchett & Datchett Solicitors. Garish headed notepaper, the name, address and details all in primary colours. Not a firm I had heard of. Based in Blackport, that was why. I felt the paper between finger and thumb. 80 gsm. Not embossed, but they never were these days; still, any half decent firm would be using 100gsm. I turned the letter to catch the light. Not even pre-printed.

"Why on earth are you using a firm of solicitors based in Blackport? It's the other end of the country."

"Malcolm recommended them."

Why? Why would he recommend solicitors working out of Blackport?

"Let's look at their website."

10 Google seconds later, the screen was filled with red, blue and yellow. At least Datchett & Datchett's website was consistent with their headed notepaper. Someone must have decided that the restrained, professional approach to website design, the pictorial equivalent of a discreet cough drawing the attention, would be less effective than a shout. And one of the messages shouted in primary colours: "RECOMMEND A RELATIVE. Recommend a relative or friend and receive £1,000."

"Did you say Malcolm recommended them to you?"

"Mr Macaw won't have done it for money. He's a solicitor."

"Maybe he knows someone good there. Strange though. Blackport is the home of the 'cash for crash' industry."

"You keep saying this 'cash for crash'. What is this?"

"It's probably what happened to your boyfriend and you. It's when a crook buys an old heap, gets you to crash into his rear by pulling away and then braking suddenly, usually at a roundabout, and then accuses you of causing the accident. They say it was originally inspired by the maze of roundabouts that encircle Blackport.

"No, it wasn't like that. We were at a petrol station, trying to get back onto the road, and Hans" (at least he was Czech then) "was sure this car slowed down and flashed his lights – I wasn't looking – so he pulled out, but the car kept going, straight into us. They said Hans pulled out without looking."

"So it was a 'flash for cash', then." I turned back to the website. " Maybe Malcolm wanted you to be able to tap into Datchett & Datchett's expertise, poacher turned gamekeeper."

She pointed at the website on the screen. "Why are you looking at these things? I am happy with Datchett & Datchett, because Mr Macaw recommended them. I just need you to sign the paper. Here."

"Let's have a look at it, then. You could be asking me to sign my life away. I once saw an agreement where one person agreed to become the slave of the other. It was a sado-masochistic relationship, between two men. Entirely illegal, of course, the agreement I mean."

"If you don't want to sign it, I'll get someone else," she said. But she did not move. I had a look. If you ignored the definitions, it was very short. Headed *'Acceptance'*.

I accept the Third Party's offer of £3,000 in full and final settlement of my claim, and I understand that I will have no further entitlement to compensation even if I suffer further symptoms or sustain further losses.

"Hmmm," I said, my approximation to a professional hmmm, "so you shouldn't accept the offer until you're sure you're better." I looked at Vessey. She was not paying attention, she was trying to bend over backwards, but her back was like a board. "You're not better, are you?"

She stood up straight. "I'm well enough," she replied.

"What if your neck injuries stop you working?"

"I already told Mr Datchett that I can't afford to stop working."

"I doubt it was Mr Datchett you spoke to. But what did they say, when you said that?"

"They said it's up to me."

"Shouldn't you ask Malcolm about this?"

"I don't want to bother him. He already did enough for me, recommending Datchett & Datchett."

"Is there another letter, one where they talk about how they arrive at the figure of £3,000?"

" 'Arrive'?" There were limits to her command of English, then.

"I mean, is there advice from the solicitors?"

"There's lots of letters. They're downstairs, in the cleaning cupboard. But I just want you to witness my signature. If you won't, I'll find someone else. I need the money."

I didn't want to let her go. So I lied. "Whoever signs it," I said, "will have to check that you know what you're agreeing to."

"Oh," she said.

"If you get me the other letters, I'll look at it all overnight and sign it tomorrow. I promise."

Overnight I would spin the straw into gold for her. I would persuade her to wait, I would turn £3,000 into £30,000, she would be eternally grateful and we would live happily ever after.

Ten minutes later she was back with a Tesco bag full of

letters.

"Tomorrow," she said, almost a threat from a flash of dark eyes under furrowed brows, as she turned and left.

I opened the bag. The correspondence was all loose, all out of date order. She was as well organised as a bag lady. "Remind me not to go to Charles University if I ever want to do a PhD," I muttered to myself.

It did not take long to get the letters into order, punch a hole in the top lefthand corner, and string them onto a treasury tag. Order to banish chaos, light to banish dark, the humble treasury tag and the hole-punch are the butler and maid to Reason.

Once the letters had been sorted out, I could see there was not much to them. The solicitors had signed her up to a 'no win, no fee' agreement, and there were reams and reams about their entitlement to costs, all in tiny print. Where was the legal advice? Here was a questionnaire:

On the scale of 1-10, what is the level of your pain? 9
How many times a week are you experiencing pain? Constantly
Is your sleep affected? Yes, I can't sleep
Are you taking medication? If so, what? Yes, painkillers
Have you consulted your GP? No
Have you attended hospital, as outpatient, as inpatient? No, no
Have you received any medical treatment? No
Has the pain stopped you working? No
How many days lost? None

Why hadn't she been to the doctor? That was a mystery, mystery number one. I moved on: but it was like almost stepping over a cliff. I was at the end of the file. All there was, was this offer. £3,000. A pre-medical offer, whatever that was. Ah, here.

> *This offer is called a pre-medical offer. That means your opponent has made an offer on the basis of the information you have given us about your injury, which we have passed on.*
> *The offer has been made without you being examined by a medical expert to ascertain the extent of your injury or its likely impact on you. As you did not attend a doctor or hospital at the time of the accident, we assume that you have suffered a minor injury. It would not be proportionate to arrange an examination by a medical expert in such a case. Accordingly, we recommend that you accept the pre-medical offer.*

What? They were telling her to accept the insurer's first offer? Before she had even seen a doctor? A minor injury? You only had to look at her, the stiff posture, the stiff movements, to realise it wasn't minor. But that was the thing: they hadn't seen her. No-one had. Why hadn't she been to the doctor herself? I would have to ask her.

Thump, step. Thump, step.

"I'm glad I'm paying you by the word," said Malcolm, surveying the papers over my desk, "because that doesn't look like typing. What is it?"

"Vessey's whiplash claim. I'm helping her with it. She wants me to witness her signature. Actually, she said you recommended the solicitors. Do they know what they're doing?"

"It's only a whiplash claim. Any fool can handle it. And it's a fool's errand to second-guess another solicitor. Unless you're being paid. Is Vessey paying you? Or is it a payment in kind you're after from our Czech beauty?" He passed me a file with a tape attached. "You won't get any kisses from me for doing this. And I don't want your opinion on it."

I looked at the cover of the file he had passed to me. 'Malcolm Macaw re. Personal Injury'.

I looked up at him. "I didn't think you handled Litigation."

"I don't." He looked red in the face. "This is my own claim, I'm the client." He pointed down to his foot. Then he turned and thump-stepped away.

I put Vessey's papers back into her plastic bag, and I opened Malcolm's file. I listened to the tape. A witness statement? That would be intriguing. I typed as I listened:

On Saturday 3rd May 2012 I parked my blue BMW 523 at the Loughton Shopping Centre car park at about 11.00am, as is my custom. I parked squarely in the parking space. I do not approve of sloppy parking. When I returned to my car after making my weekend purchases, I saw that a black Range Rover had parked so close to mine, that there was no room for me to open the driver's door. The driver was in his car and I was scolding him in moderate terms when he suddenly reversed out of the space, driving over my right foot. The pain was immediate and intense, and I was sickened by the crunch of breaking bones. The driver wound down his window and called out an insult which I do not care to repeat, before driving away. Despite my pain, I noticed his registration number which I clearly remember, OYF OFF1.

153 words. £3.06. But it was worth typing it without being paid. No wonder Malcolm had been so cagey about how he got the plastercast! How had I got the impression that it was a skiing injury? And no wonder he wanted me to type it, rather than his daytime secretary: the embarrassment,

the trickle of rumour round the office, everyone plunging into fits of the giggles every time they heard the thump-step approach.

The next item on the tape was a letter to a firm of solicitors: Michaelsons. Was he sending his witness statement directly to the solicitors on the other side? I looked in the file. Michaelsons were not acting for the other side, they were acting for him. Why not Datchett & Datchett?

Thump-step. Here was the man himself to ask.

"Because Michaelson give a bespoke service."

"What about Datchett & Datchett?"

"Off the peg. Process-driven."

"Why did you send Vessey to them, then?"

" Off the peg is good enough for a routine whiplash claim. After all, you don't want to put one of those under the full forensic glare or it might fall apart!"

I turned to him. "But they're not competent for a routine foot injury?"

He visibly bristled. "My claim is far from routine. The driver's making all sorts of wild allegations about me. Says I threatened him, says he reversed in an emergency because he feared physical harm. Nonsense."

He turned on his plastercast and hopped away. Hopping mad.

The following evening, I was looking forward to talking to Vessey about her claim. The truth is that it gave me an excuse to engage with her. She was a princess of Bohemia in an obscure Czech folktale, and I imagined her poised head crowned with a diadem, her body wrapped in a long golden gown, her spine frozen stiff by a curse. How to break the spell that bound her? I was drifting off. The truth of it was that I was finding the evening work too much. The lights glared. She was an oasis of company in this desert of solitude.

A distant roar of wind, the hoover in the last of the offices, before it attacked the central space in which my workstation sat. The roaring grew louder, and the nozzle appeared round a corner, like the trunk of an inquisitive but tentative elephant. But at the end of the trunk, it was not her. It was a man.

"Where's Vessey?"

He did not register.

"Where's the usual cleaner?"

"No no." Or was that 'no know'?

"Is she ill?"

"No know." Those may have been his only words of English.

She was back the following night. I could see her neck was rigid. She could not bend.

"You'd better sit down," I said. She had trouble. She grabbed the arms of the chair as she lowered herself into it.

"Are you okay?"

"I'm fine. It's nothing."

"It's not nothing."

"It was just one day I had to lie down. It's not so bad today. It will wear off. I have some pills."

"That's what I want to ask you about. Who prescribed the pills?"

"The doctor, of course. They are not drugs from the dealer, they are pills from the doctor." As she spoke, her brows gathered, and her eyes flashed.

"Datchett & Datchett said you didn't go to a doctor."

"I didn't go at first. In my country, you wait a year to see public health doctors, unless you bribe them to get to the front of the queue. I thought it would be the same here. I would not pay bribe, and I didn't have the money for a private doctor. But now I have found out, my friend has told me that NHS is different. I just had to register at the surgery near my street, and I saw a doctor the next day. Have you signed it, the paper?"

"You need to see a medical expert first. You've lost one day's work, and you may have to stay off work for a while so that your neck mends."

"But I want to work. I don't want to lie about all day. I don't want your compensation culture."

"But this offer of £3,000, if you lose your job, it's not enough."

"£3,000 is not enough? It is a weight of money. I am embarrassed to accept so much money. I will not ask for more."

"It's not a gift. You're entitled to it. Datchetts should have spelt out what it covers, and what it doesn't cover. And it doesn't cover time off work. You've got to ask them to send you to a medical expert."

"I won't put them to that extra expense. I have to accept the sum if they're telling me to. They are handling it out of the kindness of their hearts. They will not take any payment from me."

"Believe me, they are being paid handsomely for the work they do. They're on a 'no win, no fee'." I dug into the neat file of papers. "There," I said.

"No," said Vessey, "that's the paperwork, sure. But I think in truth they're doing it as a favour to Mr Macaw. He told me I didn't need to worry because he was going to sort it out for me so that I wouldn't have to pay anything."

"You're being taken for a ride, Vessey. Solicitors are not like that. They're a mean, grasping lot. They spend too much time telling clients what they can get away with: 'you don't need to pay this tax, you can get out of paying your employee when he's sick'. It warps them. They start trying to get away with things themselves."

"Mr Macaw's not like that. Why did he help me?"

"He's probably getting a back-hander."

"No. I'm not going to let you help me. You see only badness in everything. There is a saying in my country: don't see the oak that steals the sunlight; see the oak that offers the shade."

She pulled herself up out of the chair, hesitated, fell back with a grimace, and shuffled forward before lifting herself with her arms on the table.

"Are you okay?"

"Once I'm moving I'm okay," she said. "I have to stop taking breaks. I thank you for your help, but you are not a solicitor and that is who I must listen to."

I had an idea. I could call Datchetts myself if she agreed. Hadn't their website boasted that that their phones were manned 24 hours a day? They would agree that she must see a medical expert, when they heard she couldn't work.

"If you want to listen to a solicitor, we'll call Datchett & Datchett together, now."

She was more or less stuck in the chair, a captive audience. "Okay."

I put the phone on speaker, and dialled. The ringtone reverberated in the empty workspace. To my surprise, someone answered on the fifth tone. Vessey identified herself, and answered a security question (so, she was only 21, she acted more mature). I explained the situation. But an iron curtain fell. The answer was 'no'. No, they could not arrange for her to see a medical expert.

"Our process doesn't allow it, if the client didn't visit their GP or a hospital within 10 days of the accident."

"Why not?"

"I dunno. That's what the system says. Maybe if they didn't see a medic within 10 days, it can't have been that serious. But I dunno. I didn't write it."

"Don't you allow exceptions?"

"I can't change the parameters of the process. She's in the 'minor injuries' workflow, and once the client's in a workflow, our system won't let them be moved."

"So what's she meant to do if she's got worse?"

"Our system doesn't allow that."

"Doesn't allow her to get worse?" I could hear my voice getting louder, filling the space.

"Stop it," whispered Vessey, "don't argue with them."

"She's reached the end of the workflow. If she doesn't accept the offer that's on the table, we have to cease acting. I suppose she can go to another firm that doesn't have the 10 day rule, and start again."

I hugged my arms about my chest to contain myself. But that made me feel that I was in a strait-jacket, struggling with their mindless, arbitrary approach. I was about to let loose, when the phone went dead. Vessey had reached out and pressed the button to end the call.

"You see," she said. "Now will you sign it?"

"I can't," I said. It felt like the end of an affair. She took the folder and started to remove the papers from it.

"Oh keep the stupid folder," I said, "it's not mine, it's

the firm's."

She gave me a look of disapproval and completed the removal of the papers, which she stuffed into a plastic bag that she took from her cleaning coat. She pulled herself out of the chair, and hobbled off with her bag, to put it away. Then she returned, and the roar of the hoover filled the silence that had fallen between us. She hoovered her way out across the office, and finally, out of sight, the sound faded and died.

I found it a week later. I was passing Malcolm's office, and I heard a clarinet playing. Sonorous, sinuous. I did a double-take. It was the *Duo Concertante* by Weber, the clarinettist's composer. Did Malcolm play the clarinet too? I put my head through the door. He was out. He had said he might nip out for half an hour. There was a small pair of speakers on his desk. I stopped to listen; it was haunting in the emptiness of the deserted building. It was an enormous desk, and an enormous leather chair on the other side of it. What would it be like, being him? I moved round the desk and sat down in the chair. Luxurious. I span myself. I checked the drawers. Locked on one side, unlocked on the other. The unlocked drawer contained the usual tangle of paperclips and rubber bands, stamps and old fashioned seals and, at the back, a secret supply of chocolate bars. On his desk, a photo not of his second wife but of his second car, a big old Bentley. There were no scattered papers, he was one of those orderly workers who only ever have one file on their desk at a time. I turned to his filing tray.

The filing tray was half empty, which is how I like them, because they are only interesting after the daily filing has been done. Three types of documents remain. First, the uncategorisable, the attendance notes which relate to no particular matter. Second, the 'too difficult' pile, letters asking awkward questions that cannot be answered, phone messages from disappointed clients that cannot be returned. And third ... but as I was thinking of the categories, I was rifling though the filing tray, and my thoughts were brought to a halt as a name flashed before my eyes. I flipped back to it. A note, headed 'Attendance note':

"I recommended Vessey Zabriski to Datchett & Datchett because of their expertise," and then, added in handwriting, "for a claim of this nature" and signed with a flourish.

What an odd note to make. And how odd to sign it. What did it mean?

There is a third type of document left in a filing tray - a layer below the other two: the guilty secrets, the items of sludge that prey on the solicitor's conscience night after night, weekend after weekend, month after month.

And here was such a document. A circular from Datchett & Datchett:

Do someone a favour and earn yourself up to £5,500

If you don't handle Personal Injury work yourself, where do you send someone who consults you over an accident?

Do them a favour - and yourself — and send them to us. If we take on the case, and if the client follows our advice, we will pay you £500 plus 5% of the fees we earn, up to £5,000. You don't even need to mention the financial arrangement to the client (we will have to in our small print, but we will make it clear that it costs them nothing)

Don't tell us, tell the client *Give the client our contact details, and tell them to contact us direct. (If you contact us yourself, we can't pay you anything).*
PS Make a filenote that you recommended Datchett & Datchett because of our expertise.

Thump, step. And here was the man. I jumped up from behind his desk, and opened a filing cabinet as if I was putting something away. He stumped in, without acknowledging me, without even seeing me. Because secretaries doing the filing are invisible.

If my job at Macaws had been a permanent daytime job, I would not have said anything. If I had enjoyed my experience of working in the evening, likewise. But I had almost earned all the £1,000 I needed, and I was finding it irksome. The extra hours were making me look and feel increasingly grey and haggard in the mirror.

So I went over to the filing tray, extracted the Datchett & Datchett circular, and waved it at him.

"Touché," he said, in the voice of someone who knows the game is up. I did not need to spell it out to him.

"You know," he said, "in the old days I would have sent her to Michaelsons. It wouldn't have crossed my mind that money should change hands for passing on a client. That was part of the service. If you couldn't handle something yourself, you recommended the best person for the job. There was fat on the bone, we could afford to be gentlemanly. There were scale fees, for goodness sake!"

"Scale fees?"

"A fee scale for conveyancing: if a client was buying a property, depending on the price, our fee was a fixed percentage of that price."

"What, did the Government set the scale?"

"Not the Government, and not some independent regulator like the SRA. No, that was the beauty of it. We were self-regulated in those days, and we set the scale ourselves, the Law Society."

"So you couldn't charge more than the scale?"

"More?" He chuckled. "You couldn't charge *less* than the scale. Those were the days: clients could shop around all they liked, and they got the same price wherever they went. We weren't *allowed* to charge less. We weren't allowed to undercut another solicitor!"

Malcolm's smile faded to a wistful look, the look you might see in the eyes of an unreformed school bully remembering the fagging system from his boarding school days.

His eyes drifted back to the present. " In those days, I wouldn't have dreamt of making money out of a cleaner. Or even –" he looked at me "– paying a secretary by the word. But times are hard. It's a business now, not a profession."

"I thought solicitors are banned from paying referral fees now. Didn't the Government just change the law?"

At this, his eyes lit up. He was well and truly back from the past.

"Ah, you see I didn't *refer* her to Jim Datchett. I *recommended* him to her."

"What's the difference?"

"The Act of Parliament says I only 'refer' – he made quote marks with his fingers in the air – Vessey to Datchetts if *I* call them. I don't 'refer' her to them if *she* makes the call: that's a recommendation. When Vessey told me about her accident, I gave her Datchetts' phone number, and I recommended to her that she should phone them; I even let her use my phone. Datchetts weren't caught by the Act."

"But they paid you a referral fee."

"They paid me a 'recommendation' fee."

"*...a rose by any other name will smell as sweet.* Or in this case, will smell as rotten."

"Oh, I'm with Shylock", said Malcolm. "*What judgment shall I dread, doing no wrong?*"

"You know what became of Shylock."

"And you know what became of Romeo and Juliet."

There was a pause.

"Don't Michaelsons pay 'recommendation' fees?" I asked, using quote marks in the air as Malcolm had done.

"No. They don't look for volume." He paused. "Anyway, the important thing is that the modest gratuity I receive doesn't cost Vessey anything. It won't have come out of her compensation. Datchetts will have paid it out of their profits."

"She does pay, if she gets less compensation than Michaelsons would have got her."

"It was a bog standard claim. Datchetts won't have got it wrong."

"They have got it wrong, because they won't send her to a medical expert. You have to tell her ..."

"Too late, old boy." He looked sheepish. "She's accepted the ... what was it called ... the premedical offer."

"I don't think she has," I said. "She couldn't accept it without someone witnessing her acceptance form, and anyone who looked at it would see from the state she's in that her claim is worth more than £3,000."

"She's accepted."

"You?"

He nodded. "She wanted it witnessed. She wasn't asking for my advice. And I couldn't advise her on it; it's not my area, and if I got it wrong she could sue me. If Datchetts have got it wrong she can sue them. She was following Datchetts' advice."

"Whereas, if Vessey had rejected Datchetts' advice, you wouldn't have received your 'recommendation' fee?"

"I didn't think of that," answered Malcolm, with a half-hidden semi-smirk. "Now, if you don't mind, I'd better get on and earn some fees. And you'd better type some words. I'll be counting."

The following evening Vessey took me by surprise. There was no sound of hoovering to mark her approach. She looked dreadful, dark rings round her eyes. And she was not in her cleaning gear.

"Vessey," I said, "why are you in your coat?"

"I can't get it off. Help me."

"Here." Her back and arms were rigid, and it was a clownish pantomime as I struggled over her coat. Finally, I had full possession of it, but she was in no fit state to do two hours' cleaning. I got Malcolm to send her home. Only after I had extracted from him a promise to pay her for an evening's work. He took no persuading; he counted out a week's worth of money, but she would only take one night's, and then only under threat. It wouldn't have made much of a dent into his 'recommendation' fee even if she'd taken the week's money.

I don't know if it was Vessey's last night at Macaw & Co, but it was mine.

The next morning, to make myself feel less lousy, I took my clarinet down to Andante, the woodwind shop, to find